The Land of Artemis

The Land Of Artemis

By

CR Shuman

Lighthouse Rock Publishing
P.O. Box 18292
Sugar Land, TX 77496
www.lighthouserockpublishing.com

Cover Art: https://pixabay.com/en/castle-cloudy-mountain-2114818/

LIGHTHOUSE ROCK
PUBLISHING

This book is dedicated to my friend Matt Cordon, who got me started; to J. K. Rowling, who showed me how fun reading can be; and in memory of Jonathan Brandis, who was the inspiration for this story.

Chapter 1

The Fallen Kingdom

Once upon a time there was a great kingdom known as Artemis. This was a land full of the most beautiful animals you ever saw; unicorns, centaurs, elves, mermaids and a lot of nice people. The magic land was so beautiful that people from nearby kingdoms came to pay homage to the land and to its good and kind Queen Mary.

But cold winds brought them ill will. An evil wizard overthrew the Queen and took the kingdom for himself. His name was Morgar. He and his wife Mordra and their army took the magic kingdom and made slaves of the people and imprisoned the Queen in the dungeon. They seized her beautiful home Annis, and turned it into the dark and cold Castle Morfran, which they named after themselves. Artemis became a world of everlasting darkness.

The Queen's Royal Army tried to fight back but the wizard's army was too powerful. The last wizard in the land, whose name was Samuel, escaped with his ward Kara. Yet, trying to defend Artemis, the poor wizard was mortally wounded. He gave the rule charm to his ward and made her promise to keep the charm safe until someone from the human world came and took up the sword and charm. By so doing they could save the land and its people and overthrow the evil wizard.

Yet who would be so brave and strong to come to the aid of a mythical land?

CR&O

In the human world there lived a young boy named Chris, whose mother and father had died when he was a baby. Chris was often teased by the other kids at school because he lived in an orphanage and had an interest in magic and fantasy. Chris had no friends; even the teachers were unkind. The school itself was hard as stone, its name could bring chills down your back. The name of the school was Black Mount High. The only thing Chris wanted was to be away from his school.

One day Chris and his class went on a field trip to a very old part of town. They went in a magic shop and looked around. The owner was a young woman who looked like she was in her 20s. She said her name was Kara, and she called Chris over to her and said she had a gift for him – a gold chain charm necklace with a crystal on it. The young boy was not scared – he knew that he was meant to be there in the shop that day. The woman said to Chris, "you are very smart," and gave him the crystal charm. She then told him to come back in the morning because she had something to tell him.

The next day something weird started happening to Chris. He could move things with his mind, bend fire to his will, and even hear what people were thinking. Chris said to himself "why is this happening to me, what's going on?"

He then remembered what Kara said and he ran to the magic shop. Kara met him at the door. Chris asked "what's happening to me?....why do I have these powers?"

The good woman told him the he was the chosen one to save the magic land of Artemis.

Chris's jaw dropped.

"What?" said Chris, "I'm destined to be a warrior? You've got the wrong person, lady! I'm no hero."

"You may think not," said Kara, "but I know you are the one. I've been searching for you for so long."

She began to tell him about the fall of Artemis and the promise of the crystal charm. The more Chris listened, the more he understood, and he knew what he had to do.

So began the most epic adventure of Chris's life. He was not sure he would come back, but he knew that this land needed his help and he was willing to do all that he could to save Artemis.

Chris went home feeling different but excited.

Nothing like this had ever happen to him before.

Chris thought it be best to keep it to himself, and he did.

Chapter 2

The Lone Knight

Kara had one secret she never told anyone, not even her garden. Back in Artemis, Kara's boyfriend, Artoro, was at the mercy of Mordra.

"You, Artoro." the evil woman said. "Will you swear your loyalty to the new king of this land?"

"Never" said the brave Artoro, "I will never swear my loyalty to a man who has no right to the throne."

Then Mordra said, "Thou art exiled from this kingdom forever!"

ଓଖ୍ଠ

Chris was at school when the biggest bully in school came up to him. His name was Shark.

"What's up, stupid?" said Shark.

"Leave me alone," Chris said. Chris wanted to use his powers but Kara said not to use them for personal gain, so he just walked away.

ଓଖ୍ଠ

In Artemis, Morgar was kicking Artoro out of the once magical beautiful land. Artoro promised that he will return one day.

"This is not that day," Morgar said with an evil laugh.

ଓଖ୍ଠ

After school Chris went to the shop to see Kara.

"Hey" he said, "what's up?"

"I was just thinking about home. It's really bad back there. The people are turning into mindless drones, and the children are the evil wizard's servants. The people are his personal slaves."

Chris replied, "We will fight to take Artemis back! How do we get there?"

"See that door over there? All we have to do is walk thru it, and we will be in Artemis" said Kara. "My old friend Artoro will help us, and train you for battle, for he was exiled by Mordra."

"I'm ready, let's do it! Let's save the queen, the land, and its people!" said Chris.

Together they stepped thru the door way.

CX80

Chris could not believe his eyes.

Everything was dark. No sun at all, and the birds were not singing. All of the people of Artemis were starving and afraid. But when they saw Chris and Kara, their sadness melted away like ice.

"Where have you been?" they all said.

"I have been looking for the warrior who will save us" Kara said.

Artoro came out of the crowd and asked "who is this boy?"

Chris answered "I'm a friend of Kara, and she told me that I was the foreseen hero for whom she has been waiting."

"We will see," said Artoro. "Kara, are you sure he's the one?"

"Yes" Kara said.

"Bring me the sword of the spirit" said Artoro.

Then Chris and Artoro began to spar.

Chris never held a sword so amazingly. In all of his life, in the days that followed, Chris became more like a warrior and less like a kid.

Kara got to know her old friend Artoro again. She had always been in love with him but never told Artoro her true feelings. Since she had come home, Kara thought it was time that she come clean about her feelings. Artoro understood how she felt for he also had the same feelings for her as well.

"When can we go into battle?" said Chris.

"Very soon" said Artoro.

Morgar had a big army called the Nasties. They were very ugly creatures, some so horrible that you could not look at them.

Kara and Chris slept in a hut that Artoro had built. Even though he had been exiled, Artoro did not leave, but rather he went into hiding, and the kind people of the village all helped keep his presence a secret. The people of the local village were also very kind to Chris for having come at last. Artoro knew Kara made a good choice in finding Chris and he promised that he would be a good and wise teacher.

That afternoon Artoro helped Chris learn how to use his powers. Next to being a knight, Artoro was also a very good wizard.

"Now" said Artoro, "what am I thinking?"

"You are thinking that you, Kara and I are going to be remembered for all time for all that we have done" said Chris.

"Very good" said Artoro, "that's what I was thinking. Within a week we will take back our land and free the Queen."

At Morfran, Morgar was making life hard on Queen Mary.

"Morgar, you will never have my kingdom," she said with a brave voice.

"Oh, you will change your mind sooner than you think," said Morgar. "For I requested a treaty for you to sign stating that I, with my wife, rule this land and you will abdicate."

"Never!" said Mary.

"Then it's back to the dungeon for you!" said Morgar.

ಜಶಿ

In the village, Artoro was giving Chris a lesson before he went to bed. Since there was no more sun, it was hard to tell if it was day or night but he needed some sleep.

Artoro had one more gift to give to Chris, but he wanted to wait until he was ready. A week later Artoro knew it would be the perfect time. The next day when Chris woke up for his lesson he was shocked to find a shield sitting beside him.

Artoro came in and said, "I have watched you these past few days and thought it was the best time to give this to you."

"Oh, thank you so much," said Chris.

"It is called the Shield of Faith. With these weapons of rightness you will be able to oppose the evil wizard and his army," said Artoro.

"But what about the crystal charm?" Chris asked.

Artoro explained, "All three of them will work with the charm. Get very close to Morgar, say the spell *'forces of light empower me…restore the land its purity'*. Be strong and brave – you can defeat him."

"But how will I know when I'm ready?" asked Chris.

"When the moment comes to decide, you will know," said Artoro. "Now go to blacksmith Draco, and he will sharpen your sword."

Chris walked over to the blacksmith shop. "Ah, the young warrior. How can I help you?" asked Draco.

"I need my sword sharpened," replied Chris.

"I will be very happy to sharpen your sword, and also polish your shield," said Draco.

"Thanks a lot," said Chris and he walked back to the hut. He began to get to know the people of village.

cs⚬so

Artoro met up with him in the middle part of the village, just getting to know the people who are really friendly.

"Come now," said Artoro. "Kara wants to teach you some more spells."

"Ok," Chris said and they walked back together. It was clear that Artoro was again becoming the knight he once was.

And he was not going fail.

Chapter 3

Chris Makes a New Friend

The next day Chris was practicing his sword fighting skills when a young man came up to him.

"Hi," he said, "My name is Joseph."

"Hello," said Chris. "Artoro said I should get to know you."

Joseph was a tall red-headed young man with very strong arms. At the time of the attack he was studying with Artoro, but when the good knight was exiled he gave up on his studying. So when Joseph heard about Chris he knew he should get back on track and spar with the young warrior.

"So," said Joseph, "want to try your hand with me?"

"Sure," Chris said.

Joseph gave the first blow. Chris ducked then swung his sword. Joseph fell backwards.

They ran back and forth, both swords clashed this way and that. Finally the two boys tired, settled on a victor – Joseph.

Chris was very impressed. He had never seen such swordsmanship.

"Well, you are very good with the blade."

"Thank you," said Joseph.

After that they started talking and getting to know each other.

"So tell me," asked Chris, "how long did you train with Sir Artoro?"

"Up until the war came to Artemis." Joseph said.

"That's cool," said Chris. He then told Joseph about growing up.

"I lived in an orphanage. My mom and dad were killed in a car crash when I was a baby, so I was sent to live in the orphanage when I was 5 years old."

Hours passed by quickly as they talked.

Artoro came by and greeted the two boys.

"Have you two been sparring together?" he asked.

"Yes," they said in unison.

"I thought you would make good friends." said Artoro, and smiled.

"Well, come along. Kara has dinner ready."

They both raced to the hut and ate like kings.

⋘⋙

At Morfran, Mordra was having a little girl of only seven years clean her feet and paint her nails. Her name was Frieda, and she dared not speak for fear she might be put into the hot box.

"Faster!" said Mordra.

The poor girl started to cry as she painted the evil woman's nails.

⋘⋙

At the village, Joseph and Chris made their beds and talked all night. They were becoming like brothers. They decided to do some more sparring the next day after Chris had his lesson with Kara.

In the morning Chris and Joseph went to their lesson.

"Today," said Kara, "we are going to learn how to transform enemies into cups." She began their instruction.

"One, two, three, this is stupid," said Joseph.

"Oh well, what kind of spell would you like learn?"

"How about how to talk to snakes?" Joseph said.

"Okay," Kara said, "but next time Joseph, mind your tongue. I'm your teacher. Just because you are studying to be a knight and wizard does not mean you can get your own way."

"I'm sorry," said Joseph.

"I don't mind learning how to talk to snakes," said Chris.

"Ok, then let's begin the lesson."

They were in class all day before the boys got some free time and did some sparring. The practice helped Chris prepare for the battle that was coming.

"You know, Chris, if this works out, maybe after the war you can stay here."

"That would be very cool, and I would like that" said Chris.

"Well, that's all for today." said Kara. "Off you boys go! See you tomorrow!"

And they ran to do some sword fighting.

"So, how did someone like you get a teacher like Artoro?" asked Chris.

"Well, like you, I never knew my mother or father. Sir Artoro took me in and raised me as his own showed and me everything about being a knight."

"That's very cool," said Chris. "Do you think I can stand up to Morgar?" Chris asked.

"I think you have what it takes to spar with me....don't you?" asked Joseph.

"Yes, but that's different," said Chris. "That's for training and for fun."

"But at least it gets you ready for the battle ahead," Joseph said. "And I could not think of anyone I could spar with or fight with better than you," said Joseph.

"Thanks," said Chris. "You are a good friend Joseph. You are a very nice person," said Chris.

"I feel the same way," Joseph said.

Just then Artoro came walking up.

"Hello, boys," he said. "How has your day been so far?"

"Ok," they said. "We were just chatting."

Well, that is all for today. You need to rest," said Artoro.

"Ok." they said. The boys quickly removed their armor.

But that night, both of them stayed up late and talked.

"How did Morgar get to be so evil?" Chris asked.

"Well, they say he was abandoned by his mother because of what he could do. He lived in the darkness of the woods and learned what he could on his own until he was rescued."

"So why does he want Queen Mary's kingdom?" asked Chris.

Joseph sighed. "Morgar and Mary are half brother and sister, and Morgar is mad because Mary inherited the throne when their father died. His mother Aveline was a commoner. King William fell in love with her long before he met Mary's mother, who was the child of a foreign king and their marriage arranged. So poor Aveline gave birth to the commoner baby, and almost immediately he began to show some strange abilities. But because he was born out of wedlock, and she feared his abilities, she abandoned him. The child was rescued and raised by Celtics who taught him to use his magic. And now Morgar wants the throne because he is first born. As the years went by, Morgar grew more and more angry and thought the throne should be his, and he vowed to claim it."

Chris was in awe as Joseph told him everything he knew about Morgar.

"How could a good king like William disown his own son just because of his lowly birth?" asked Chris.

It would be only a matter of time before Artemis' fate would be decided, and the question of who would rule the land would be answered.

Chapter 4

An Unforgiving Past

At Morfran, Morgar went to see Mary in her dungeon cell.

"How are you?" he said with an ugly look on his face.

"How do you think I am?" said Mary. "No matter what you do to me I will never sign the abdication, and you will never have my throne," she said with a determined look.

At that Morgar said, "I am the first born…..the throne shall be mine."

"It's not my fault that our father did not accept you as ruler and put out your mother, and then married my mother", said Mary.

"No," said Morgar. "But you are the reason I'm not king. You were father's favorite. He gave you everything and left me nothing."

Mary fought back and said, "You are too cold and unfeeling. Why did I have to have a cold-hearted brother like you?"

"Just lucky, I guess." said Morgar with evil smile.

"You can't keep me here forever!" said Mary.

"Oh, I think I can," Morgar said calmly, with a sneer. "And you can rot in here until you see things my way, my sister."

And he left with a laugh.

Mary sat down and prayed that help would come soon, and that her army was getting ready.

And they were.

Every day Draco was making swords and armor. It was as if to say *'we are coming, Mary….. have faith and hope! Morgar will not win, and he does not have faith and hope and he will never know love or friendship!'*

In her cell Mary prayed for her kingdom to be saved one day and for her people, and for the army being built for battle. Mary also felt sorry for Morgar, deep within her cell, and she prayed for her half-brother even though he was the way he was. With her pure heart, the queen still loved her brother.

Morgar, on the other hand, did not have any love for his sister nor anyone else. Morgar had no heart but a block of ice within him.

Morgar had a personal guard whose name was Maxims. He was big and strong and very hot tempered, and if you made him mad he would challenge you to a fight, and Maxims would always win. He even smelled bad, and didn't even brush his teeth.

Morgar was very fond of him and was impressed with his strength.

Morgar loved to see the people be weak and without food. The Nasties would do what they wanted, which usually was terrorizing the young girls of the village. And Morgar had begun taxing the heart and soul out of the poor people of Artemis.

CXBO

That night while Chris was asleep he had a confusing dream. He dreamed that Queen Mary came to him and told him, *"the time is at hand.....you must come soon."*

Chris awakened as if he had received a vision from God. The next day, Chris told Artoro and Joseph about his dream.

"How odd!" they exclaimed.

"Why did I have this dream, but no one else did?" asked Chris.

"Maybe the Queen has faith that you will come for her and rescue her people," said Joseph.

"I'm glad that Queen Mary has such strong hope for me," said Chris.

"So do I," said Joseph.

"My advice to you, Chris," said Artoro, "is to listen to your dream…..listen to what is being said in your dream."

"Maybe you are right." said Chris. "Maybe I should listen to my dream."

That night Queen Mary came to him in a dream a second time, and said the same thing. *"The time is at hand…..come soon…..I wait on thee!"*

"Two times in a row…..that really means something!" Chris said to himself. "Artoro and Joseph are right…..I should listen to my dream!"

CƷ🙰

The next morning he went to see Kara about his magic.

"I was wondering," said the young wizard in training, "if you could teach me how to fly?"

"Well," said Kara. "I hope you mean without a broom. Think of yourself floating and being lifeless......it will happen."

As Mary was speaking, Chris' feet began to lift off the ground. At first he was scared, but then the young wizard gathered his thoughts and said in his young modern voice, "This is so cool!"

"Now if you want down," said Kara, "think of being on the ground."

So Chris closed his eyes and he was on the ground.

"So that's all there's to it?" asked Chris.

"Yes, that is all it is" said Kara with a smile.

"Cool….thanks!" said Chris excitedly.

ᏪᏃ

At Morfran, Mordra was having one of the children draw her bath. The little girl walked over to tub fearfully, and began to pour the water.

"Thank you, child," she said with an evil smile. "Now leave, and mop my bedroom."

The poor girl left and mopped the bedroom floor, crying as she mopped.

In the throne room Morgar was making battle plans.

"Where are these little wizards hiding?" he said with an evil sneer. "If only I could find their hideout, I could trap them where they are. But where is it?" Morgar said to himself.

Just then the evil wizard had an idea. He would trick one of them into telling him where they were now.

"Who could it be?" he wondered, then a thought came to him. "I will ask that blacksmith!" Morgar said, laughing his head off.

So the plan started to take shape in his evil little mind, and the next day he made sure it was carried out. He went into the village disguised as a hermit. Morgar walked very slowly so that nobody knew it was him.

CB&O

Chris loved his sword, and thought it was the most beautiful thing he had ever owned. Anxious to see what all it could do, he left the village to walk in the woods. While walking, he used his sword to hack at bushes and weeds and anything that was in his way. The shiny sharp sword made it so very easy.

Suddenly he felt himself being swooped up into the air. Before he knew it, he was trapped in a heavy net, hanging from a tree. Trying to figure out what had happened, he saw a group of little people jumping and cheering beneath him. They were dressed all in green and wearing clothes made from leaves and twigs.

"Let me down!," he demanded.

One of the elves stepped forward.

"No! We will not free you! Not until you promise to stop destroying our beautiful forest. This is our home, and we need the trees and bushes to live. Swear you will stop!"

Chris took a deep breath.

"I swear."

He saw two of the elves unwinding the rope from a nearby tree, and felt his heavy trap being lowered to the ground. As he laid quietly on the ground, the speaking elf stood over him.

"You are not free yet, for you must stand before our king to account for your actions."

They tied his hands behind his back and with his own sword, they prodded him to walk through the woods until he came to a village square. All of the houses and benches were tiny, just the right size for elves.

Sitting on a stone in the center, with an elf warrior on either side was their king. He was dressed in a leather cape and trousers, and held a staff in one hand.

"Step forward and tell me your name."

Chris stood before him, and spoke.

"My name is Chris and I am from the Modern World. I was brought here by Kara to fight Morgar and the Nasties, and to take back Artemis!"

The king thought for a moment, then he spoke.

"My name is Hegewith, and these people are Minkals. We have no dealings with Artemis, but we don't want Morgar and the Nasties to destroy our home, which we know they will do if they are not stopped. There are too few of us to help with the fight, but we can give you our two most valued possessions which we believe will be of use. We will loan you our two magic capes, which were given to us by the wizard Samuel. Whoever wears the capes will become invisible. Please use them, and bring them back to us as a symbol of your victory."

Just then one of the Minkals stepped forward and handed Chris a leather pouch.

"Thank you, King Hegewith. I will work very hard with the good people of Artemis to keep your village and your people safe."

With a bow, he turned and let the Minkals lead him back to the village path.

಄಄

At Kara's hut Chris and Joseph were sparring and having a good time doing it.

"Ah! Got you again!" said Joseph.

"Oh, you think so?" said Chris. He raised his sword, and with power the sword came down like an axe. Joseph then blocked his attack, but Chris made him fall under his shoes.

"Ah, got YOU!" Chris said. "You can't beat me!"

"I must say," Joseph said, "you have been training harder."

Then they heard footsteps.

"Hello," came the voice of an old man. It was Morgar in disguise.

"You two have good fighting skills."

"Thank you!" they said. "We are training for battle against the evil wizard Morgar.

"Oh, do you think you can beat him?"

"No." said Chris, "but we can try."

And with that Morgar walked away with an evil smile under his hood.

Chapter 5

Chris Gets a New Power

A month had gone by, and Artoro thought it was time to test Chris' skills in combat. Chris would also receive one last power. Morphing was a very old power in Artemis. Only the most powerful wizards had it, and Artoro was one of them. He sent Joseph to get Chris and tell him about the test he was about to take place.

"Well," said Artoro, "are you ready for the test?"

"Yes," said Chris. "What do you want me to do?"

"Just walk into that cave over there and deal with what you will find there."

"What will I find?" Chris asked.

"Fear." said the brave knight. "And when you come out I have a gift for you, my young pupil."

So Chris went into the cave cautiously, but he was sure he would make it out, no matter what happened. With a big deep breath Chris walked in further. The cave was very dark and misty inside. "I wish I had a flashlight," he told himself. At that moment a flashlight was in his hand.

"Who dares shine light in my house?" said a voice in the darkness.

"It is Chris, Warrior of Artemis."

Chris walked around a corner and saw a dragon.

"Come closer," said the beast.

"Ah, so you are the young warrior I have heard so much about. I am Kilgore, the great dragon of Artemis."

"So am I to face you?" said Chris.

"Yes," said the dragon, "but without fear."

"I am very scared, but I will fight you," said Chris.

He took out his sword and prepared to fight. Kilgore attacked first. The dragon got the boy on the arm. Chris fought back and chopped off one of his horns. Kilgore shot his fire, Chris blocked his attack with his shield. The battle went on and on until at last the final blow came from Chris's own sword. Both out of breath and still alive, the two of them fell back.

"Artoro has taught you well," said Kilgore. "Are you still afraid of me, boy?"

"No." said Chris. "Not anymore."

"Then you have passed the test and lost your fear," said Kilgore. "God speed, good warrior." And the great dragon backed away into the darkness.

Chris felt braver and less like a young boy and more like a man as he walked out of the cave.

"Well done, my friend," said Artoro. "You have earned the power of morphing."

"Oh wow," said Chris. "I have always wanted to change myself," Chris said with a surprised look on his face.

"All you have to do," said Artoro, "is to think of an animal and you turn in to that animal. As long as you remember to turn back into a human and have control of your human mind. If you don't, you will be trapped as the animal of your morphing."

"Wow," said Chris, "that's a lot to think about, but I will be careful and heed the warning you gave me."

"See that you do," said Artoro. Chris and Joseph walked back to their hut that night with brave hearts.

"Goodnight," said Joseph.

"Goodnight," said Chris.

Chris went to bed feeling braver than he ever been in his whole life.

Chapter 6

God Reveals Himself to Chris

The next day Chris woke up ready for anything. Kara had breakfast made.

"Eat up! You are going to need it where you and Artoro are going."

"Where are we going?" Chris asked.

"Well," said Kara, "Artoro has something special planned for today so eat up and you can go get Joseph after that."

Chris ate like a tornado and then ran to get Joseph.

"Hi, Joseph," said Chris.

He told Joseph that Artoro had something special planned for them so on they walked.

"Good morning, young wizards," said Artoro with very happy smile on his face. "Well, let's get going."

And off they went.

Artoro told the boys that they were going to a special place where he went when he was a wizard in training.

"We worked on getting over fear. Now Chris, it's time to find your inner spirit."

Chris's jaw dropped.

"My inner what? I did not know there was a spirit in me."

Artoro laughed.

"Not a spirit in you! I mean your inner self," Artoro said.

"Today we are going to a special lake named Rosebud. It's as clear as glass and the water there is very pure," said Artoro.

They rode for hours then at last they came to the lake. Chris got down from his horse and was in awe at the sight of the lake. It really was clear as glass. Chris said quietly, "I'm going for a walk by myself alone."

Chris went alone down a hill and came upon a meadow. There he began to think about the things he done back home at the orphanage. One thing came to mind. Chris thought of the time when Shark was trying to hit him and Chris pushed Shark all the way to the school playground. He wished he had gone to the office and told the principal and not have taken matters in own hands. So after his walk and careful thought, Chris was ready.

I wonder what I have to do, he asked himself.

When Chris got back to the lake, he told Joseph and Artoro that he was ready.

"Good," said Artoro. "Now walk into the lake and wait."

"Wait for what?" Chris asked. But he did as he was told, and walked into the cool water until it was up to his waist.

Artoro did not answer. He just stood there and waited with Joseph. But just when all seemed hopeless, a voice from above spoke clearly.

"Chris, my child, I have heard your prayer. Do you forgive the boy who wronged you? Do you forgive everyone who wronged you?"

"Yes," Chris said.

"And do you forgive yourself for pushing Shark? Do you forgive yourself for all of the times you were angry?" the voice asked again.

"Yes, but….," Chris stuttered, "who are you?"

"I am your Heavenly Father. I have known you since you were created, I have loved you, and I have always been with you and watched over you."

Chris went silent. He had never been to church, which is what he thought God was for. But then finally the words came out.

"Father," said Chris, "I ask for your forgiveness and want be your child."

"My son," the voice replied, "I love you very much. I forgive you for all your sins."

Chris bowed his head. "Thank you, Lord."

Chris walked out of the lake feeling blessed and humbled.

Chapter 7

The Eve of Battle:
The beginning of the end

The next day Chris woke up and found Artoro outside.

"Good morning," Artoro said.

"Morning," Chris said. He yawned loudly. "Where are Joseph and Kara?" Chris asked.

"They went to get your new armor ready," Artoro answered with a smile.

Chris almost fell over with an excited look on his face.

"Oh, Master Artoro!" Chris said. "Really?"

"At last. Yes, my young knight, it's time to prepare for battle," Artoro said. "Over the next two days, Chris, I will train you for combat."

Artoro then told him that Morgar would use anything to trick him.

"So you must be careful."

Chris nodded in agreement.

Later that day, Joseph and Kara came with Chris's new shiny armor.

"It looks great!" Chris said, overwhelmed and smiling.

The armor was made of hard steel and shined in the sunlight. The helmet and breastplate were adorned with the holy cross. Chris tried the armor with help from Joseph.

"You look magnificent," Joseph said.

"Thanks," Chris said in gratitude.

Later that afternoon Artoro addressed the villagers of Artemis.

"In three days we will go in to battle and fight not for just ourselves but for the freedom of the great land of Artemis, and in the name of our marvelous and beautiful queen. Let all of Artemis know that our great army is awakening, and that Morgar will regret the day that he ever set a foot on our great land."

The people cheered.

Artoro had one last thing to ask.
"I ask sons, fathers, brothers, sisters, and mothers – all who are able bodied – to join us in our quest for Victory!"

"Yes!" They all said with applause.

Artoro and the others were very proud of how the people were willing fight by their side and die for them.

"And may God bless and protect us all!" Chris cried out with a voice of a warrior.

"Then, my fellow warriors," Artoro said, "train hard and be ready! And now, let us pray."

Artoro bowed his head, and prayed silently for victory and safety. The villagers joined him in their own silent prayers.

"Goodnight to you all!" Kara said happily.

That night all of Artemis slept with courage in their hearts.

Chapter 8

Evil Forces Plot Their Revenge

It was three days before the final battle, and Morgar was talking to his blacksmith.

"How are the swords and the armor coming along?" Morgar asked.

"Very well my lord," the blacksmith said. "Both the swords and armor are ready."

"Good. Very good," Morgar said with an evil smile. "Now show me how they work."

"Yes my lord," said the blacksmith." The armor is of pure black iron. Fire and lighting bolts can't harm them. Not even glass," the blacksmith said. "And the swords can cut through the hardest armor and helmet."

"Good, good," said Morgar. "Now our army will be indestructible."

Cʒʒɔ

In the village Chris and the others were also preparing for the upcoming battle.

"Nice move," said Joseph.

"Thanks," said Chris. "I had a good teacher."

At that moment the teacher was coming to see how their sparring was coming along.

"Hail, and well met fellow knights!" said Artoro. "How's the training coming along?"

"It's awesome!" said Chris." And my new armor is cool too. I feel so powerful."

"So do I," Joseph said with a smile. "My armor is very cool too, as my new friend states….with the image of the lion on the breastplate."

Artoro smiled. "We are all now warriors of God."

"And may the Lord protect us," said Kara who had just came out the hut after making breakfast for them. "Come on and eat. All of you. You'll need your energy to fight."

Kara had already eaten when they all finished sparring.

"So what's for breakfast?" Chris asked as they came in.

"Eggs, toast, and bacon." said Kara.

Later that day Chris was taking a walk and watching all the people working hard and training for the battle. Chris saw the hope in their eyes, and it felt good to him to know that these people were willing to fight by his side and even die with him, no matter the cost. Chris, Joseph, and Artoro knew the three days would be hard but they were not afraid.

"With God on our side we can do anything, and nothing can stop us," said Joseph.

 CRBO

At Morfran, Mordra was talking to her one of her spies.

"Go down into the village and see what's happening and discover their plans. Go now and report back to me when you are done," said Mordra, with an evil smile.

The spy left quickly, putting on a hood as he departed.

CRBO

Joseph and Chris were sparring when they saw the hooded man.

"Hello…may we help you?" Chris asked.

"Yes, I'm looking for a place to stay for several nights."

"Are you with us?" asked Joseph excitedly, but Chris was worried. He wondered from where this man had come.

Chapter 9

Chris Does Some Searching

The next day was so very cold. All of the village and warriors stayed inside their homes, sitting by the fire.

Chris was watching the man carefully, who said his name was Fox, talking to Artoro and Kara about joining the army and the fight. Chris was reading Fox's mind. It was hard at first but after a while it was easier. And what Chris heard and saw in Fox's mind was not good.

Chris tried to tell Artoro, Kara, and Joseph, what he had learned – that Fox was a spy working for Mordra. They did not believe him, so Chris went to his room to pray.

"Help me make them believe me," Chris prayed silently. "One way or another."

Then Chris got an idea.

That evening as the village slept, Chris morphed into a fly and flew to the cottage were Fox was staying. Chris was amazed to find out that the table in Fox's cottage was covered with technology devices, things that came from the modern world.

Fox opened up a video link on his handheld device, and told Morgar all that he learned.

"Hello, my lord. Things are going as planned," said Fox with a gleeful smile.

"Well," said Morgar, "what have you found?"

"They have given the boys new armor and swords that can turn invisible. The swords can cut through the hardest armor."

"And what about the battle?" asked Morgar.

"Their army grows every day. They bring them in from other kingdoms. The plan is to take a secret path in the mountains and catch you unaware."

"Good, good, Fox. You have done well," said Morgar.

"Thank you, your highness," Fox said.

"I better go…they will wonder where I am."

So Fox turned off his device and walked out of the cottage.

Chris flew out of the cottage with Fox, then hid behind a large tree where he morphed back into a human form. "I must tell the others. Then they will believe me now," Chris said, running towards the hut.

"Wake up, everyone! I have something important to tell you!"

"What is it?" asked Kara sleepily.

"Fox has technology from the modern world and he uses it to communicate with Morfran. I have a recording of what Fox told Morgar."

"We might as well listen.....there will be no peace until we do," said Joseph.

"Ok," said Artoro, "let's hear the recording."

Chris took out the tape recorder and started the recording, and the others listened.

"Well," said Artoro, "there goes our surprise attack. We need to think of a new battle plan."

"I second that," said Kara.

"Then it's settled," Chris said, "we will think of a new plan tomorrow."

"Ok," Artoro said. "Everyone, get some sleep."

"Goodnight, everyone," Joseph said, and all fell fast asleep.

Chapter 10

We Have a Plan

The next day Chris awoke with a start. He had an idea, so he went to the village hall and called for a meeting.

"Friends, fellow knights, in order for our victory to be complete" he announced. "we must free the queen before we can take back Artemis."

"How will we do that?" Joseph asked with a puzzled look.

"Well," said Chris with a sly grin, "the capes from the Minkals will become very handy. We will give them to two spies who will sneak in and search for our Queen Mary. "

"And get information about their battle plans, and learn their weaknesses," said Joseph. "Then we can use what we found out on our side instead."

"What great idea!" exclaimed Kara. "They won't know what they cannot see."

"The final battle is at hand," said Chris. "In two days we will go to war and as I have said before, we fight not only with swords but with the power of the Holy Spirit. Prepare your hearts and your bodies within these two days. You now fight in God's army," said Chris with a voice that was as clear as the sea.

"Yes, let us sleep now and tomorrow have the power to do what we came here to do. We are willing and able to fight and die for you and for our great land!" shouted a voice in the crowd. Soon, others began to cheer.

"That's what I hoped you'd say, so goodnight to you all and sleep well," Chris responded.

Chapter 11

Getting Ready for Battle

Two days just before the final battle Artoro asked Chris and the rest of the army to come forward and gather around him for prayer.

"Most godly men, tomorrow we go in to battle, but tonight we pray and dance before the lord like king David did before us."

"Oh most great and loving Father," Said Artoro. "We come to you and ask you to be with us in the coming battle, and help us overcome the evil Morgar, and save our queen Mary. Please be with our hero and second command of the army. In Your Son's name, Amen."

"Artoro, why did you call me second in command?" Chris asked with a puzzled look on his face.

"Because I'm only the captain. The army will only listen to you," said Artoro with obedience in his voice.

"Ok," said Chris, "tomorrow we go in to battle, but tonight we feast and pray for a great victory."

With hope in their hearts the army swore their loyalty to Chris and his captain.

"I will try to be a good leader," said Chris to his army.

And with that they went to bed.

And when the morning came, Chris called Artoro and his army together.

Chapter 12

Let the Final Battle Begins

It came to pass that the day of the final battle came to Artemis. Chris was getting ready, but he was also thinking of what to say to the people to lift their spirits. All of the hopes now rested with him, and he was surprised to be afraid.

It was a new afternoon when Joseph came to check on him and see if Chris needed any help.

"Can I help you with your armor?" Joseph asked.

"Yes, thanks," said Chris a look of worry on his face.

"What's the matter?" Joseph asked.

"Well, in less than an hour we go in to battle, and I don't know what to say to them."

"Well," said Joseph, "just say what you feel. Take a deep breath and let it out."

"You are right," Chris said, and walked to meet the villagers of Artemis.

"Today we fight a battle as old as time and for the future of our land and our Queen. Should we win the day, it will be remembered for generations to come. We fight not only for the kingdom but for our freedom. We are fighting for our right to live. Like I said before, our children and our children's children will talk about this for years to come. For the love of Artemis and for the love of our Lord and also our Queen. Let us pray now that God be with us in battle. Bring us back our land and our Queen. Will you fight with me?"

"Yes!" they yelled.

"Will you die with me?"

"Yes!" they yelled.

"Then in the name of our Queen, and the name of the Lord, follow me!"

They rode all day and all night until at last they came to the once beautiful and powerful castle of Queen Mary, now dark and covered with vines.

Chris took a deep breath and said, "Let the acting ruler of Artemis come forth! To let justice be done on him according to the laws of the land!"

"I am the king here!" exclaimed Morgar with an evil smile from the castle wall, high above the army. "My sister is the pretender to the throne. I'm the true heir to the throne. I will not bow to you or to her!" Morgar said with an evil voice.

"Then you leave me no choice. Tonight, we go to war!" Chris said.

"When darkness turns to light, it ends!"

For the love of Artemis and for Queen Mary, the two armies met on Stargazer Field below Mount Artemis. Swords were clashing there and here.

But meanwhile the spies, cloaked in the magic capes, were sneaking in to rescue the queen.

Morgar had the queen's army cornered but just when all seemed lost Chris used all his powers of the Crystal Charm and said the magic words, *"forces of light empower me restore this land to it's purity."*

With all of his energy he walked over to the now wounded Morgar.

"Go ahead," he groaned with a weak voice, "be a man, kill me."

"I'm not going to kill you," Chris said. "Your life is not mine to take." He turned to the Queen coming up a hidden set of stairs, newly released from her dark dungeon cell by the spies.

"What do you think we should do with him, Queen Mary?"

"Let him live," said the Queen. Then she turned to Morgar. "You are my brother. You will be banished from the land forever. You and your wife leave here today."

₧トდ

"Chris, Joseph, Artoro, and Kara…stand before me." said the Queen with a smile.

"Kneel down." The four brave leaders knelt with their heads bowed.

"I, Queen Mary, ruler of Artemis, hereby knight you all as members of my court," said the queen.

"And you Chris, we owe such gratitude to you for saving everyone and my kingdom. What is your heart's desire?" asked Queen Mary.

"Well," said Chris, "I would like to live here in Artemis with Kara and Artoro forver, but there's something I must do first."

And with wave of her hand, she sent Chris back at the shop. From the window he could see Shark beating up a seventh grader.

"Hey!" Chris yelled, "leave him alone!"

"Or what?" said Shark.

"Or this," Chris said. With a powerful look on his face and with a wave of his fist Shark went flying off his feet. Chris then picked up the stunned bully by his shirt collar.

"Put me down!" Shark cried.

"Oh, did you say down?"

With a thud Shark came down hard.

"Ouch!" said Shark crying as he hit the ground.

"Thank you," said the young boy.

"You're welcome," said Chris.

"Now Shark, be off with you or I will call the cops." Shark ran up the street.

Chris returned to Artemis, and lived happily as a knight and young wizard, and had many more adventures, but that's another story.